CARRY ME ALONG!
Om
DINOSAURS

The T-rex would roar loud and strong,

Look, there are some dino eggs! How many can you spot?

This Dino King's jaw was 4-foot long!

The mighty Stegosaurus would be ready to attack,

With a spiked tail and flat plates on its back!

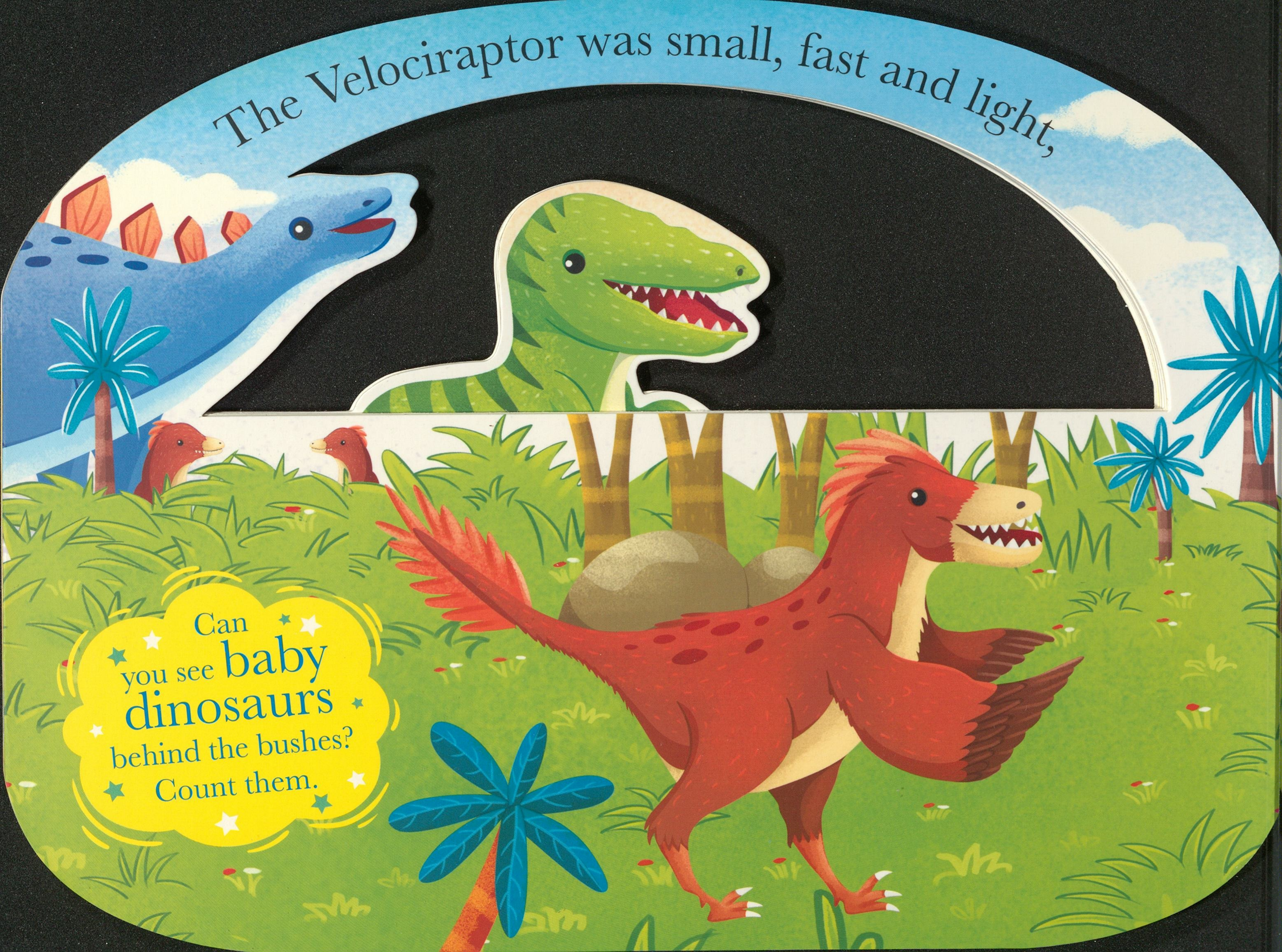

The Velociraptor was small, fast and light,

Can you see **baby dinosaurs** behind the bushes? Count them.

Despite its feathers, it couldn't take a flight!

On its skull the Triceratops had a frill of bone,

For its three horns and bird-like beak it is known!

Spot the **three horns** of the Triceratops!

In the water the Spinosaurus would find its prey,

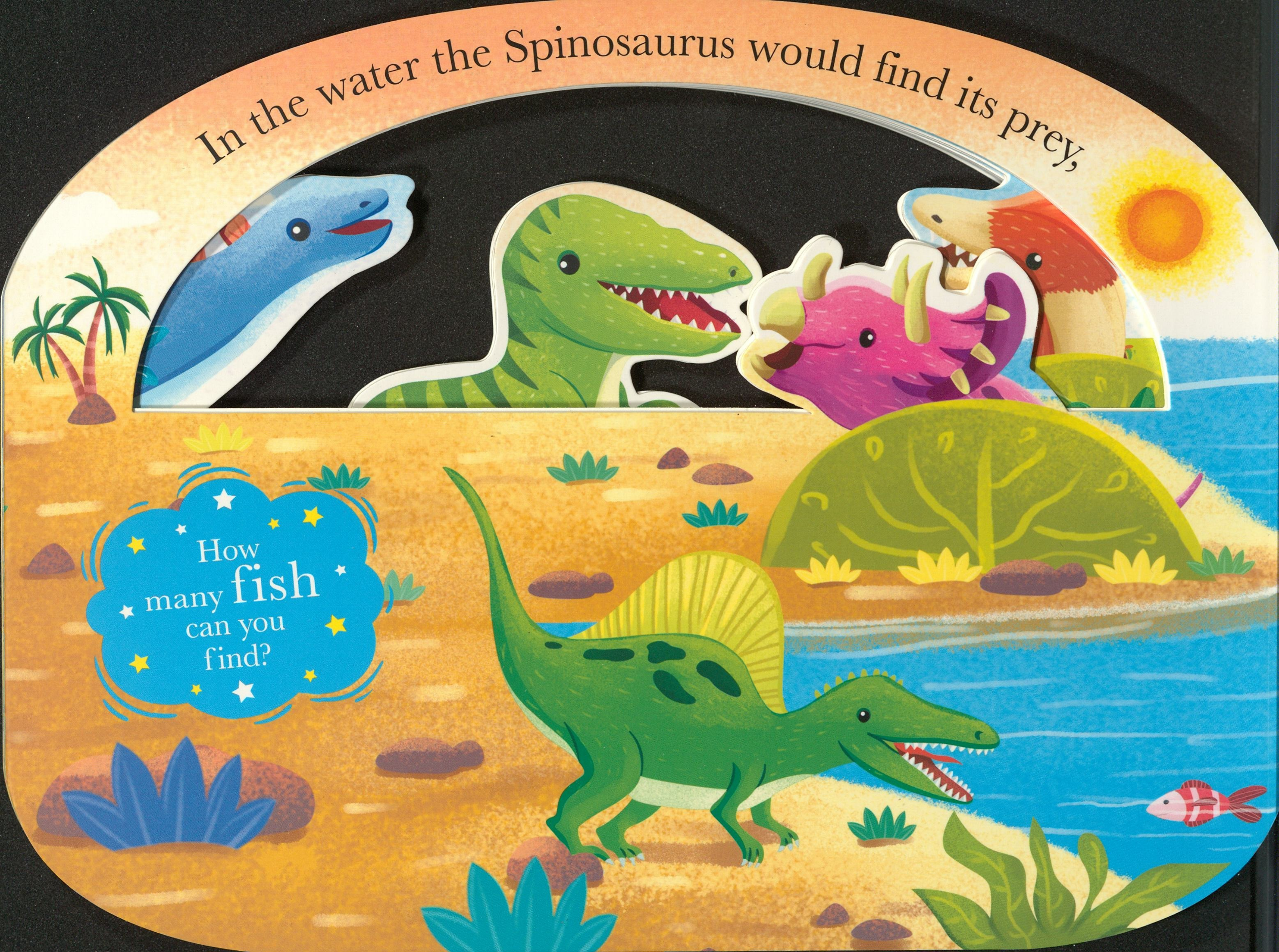

How many **fish** can you find?

With the sail on its back it could swim away!

CARRY ME ALONG!

T-rex, Velociraptor and many more! Enjoy the rhymes, busy scenes, learn about different kinds of dinosaurs and respond to the prompts on each page of this wonderful book that comes with a "carry along" handle.

First Published in 2024

Om Books International

Corporate & Editorial Office
A-12, Sector 64, Noida 201 301,
Uttar Pradesh, India
Phone: +91 120 477 4100
Email: editorial@ombooks.com
Website: www.ombooksinternational.com

ISBN: 978-81-96043-66-7

Printed in China

10 9 8 7 6 5 4 3 2 1

Sales Office
107, Ansari Road, Darya Ganj,
New Delhi 110 002, India
Phone: +91 11 4000 9000
Email: sales@ombooks.com

CE

ISBN 978-81-960436-6-7
US $ 9.99 £ 8.50
Om KIDZ
9 788196 043667
www.ombooksinternational.com
00039500

ombooksinternationalofficial
ombooksinternational
ombooksdelhi